Ashford Lindsay

Memoir of Miss Elizabeth McQuerns

Ashford Lindsay

Memoir of Miss Elizabeth McQuerns

ISBN/EAN: 9783337202408

Printed in Europe, USA, Canada, Australia, Japan

Cover: Foto ©Raphael Reischuk / pixelio.de

More available books at **www.hansebooks.com**

MEMOIR

—OF—

MISS ELIZABETH McQUERNS

—BY—

—MRS. M. A. LINDSAY—

DUE WEST, S. C. :
"ASSOCIATE REFORMED PRESBYTERIAN" PRINT.

1887.

IN MEMORIAM.

In this feeble and imperfect sketch of an eminently useful woman, I shall refrain from eulogy, beyond that which falls spontaneously from pen and lips, when those who knew her best write or speak of her. As relative, teacher and friend she is associated with my earliest recollections, and for the past eighteen years a beloved and revered inmate of my home ; therefore it has seemed, by those most interested and best capable of judging, "not unseemly" that upon me should devolve the mournful task of thus in some degree commemorating her character and virtues.

It is with a sorrowful heart that I recognize and try to measure my own personal loss and, I doubt not, that hundreds of pupils and friends from every section of our country, and even in the "regions beyond," will unite with me in the desire to keep her "memory green" and to cull from it for our guidance something of the virtues it exemplified, so that "though dead she may yet speak."

The memory of the JUST is a heritage of priceless value. Emphatically may this grand title be applied to our beloved friend. Length of days through a kind Providence was hers, in which to teach the great lesson of faithfulness to duty, and by the same gracious Benefactor she was well equipped for its performance. Endowed with a heart permeated with desire for usefulness, a benevolence superlatively self-denying, industry unwearied and unintermittent, talents which though not the favored servant's allotment were yet so invested as to yield an exceptionally satisfactory evidence of profitable stewardship, a constitution that carried her through three generations with a comparatively small modicum of pain or serious illness, and a childlike spirit whose trust was unwavering—what wonder that her life was a benediction ?

ELIZABETH McQUERNS was the youngest child of Samuel and Bettie (Thompson) McQuerns, both of whom were natives of Ireland. Whether married before or after their emigration to this country we do not know. Among my own family records are dismissions of ancestors from the church of which her parents were members.. Written in the quaint style of the period, they, with the substitution of different names, are no doubt literal copies of those granted to her parents, and as illustrative of her godly ancestry, and as an old-time relic, one of these is transcribed :

"We the undersigned perfons do certify that we have known the bearer —— —— and his wife and family upwards of nine years, who have all behaved themfelves Honeftly, Soberly and Inoffensively and may All be Received into any Protestant Decenting congregation in the Universe for anything ever heard of or known by us.

"Given under our hand this 27th September, 1787, at Clough, County Antrim, Ireland.

Elders,	Pastor,
Thos. Gaston,	Rev. Joseph Duglass.
Robt. Boyd,	
Nash White.	

It was then the latter part of the year 1787 that her grandparents, parents, and a colony, amongst whom were the Fairs, Thompsons, Adgers, Drennans, and other families well known in this country, came over as passengers in the same ship. Several of these settled in Newberry District, and connected themselvs with the Associate Reformed Church at Cannon's Creek. In that County she was born March 8th, 1802.

Her recollections of these infant years were indistinct. Unlike many of the aged whose garrulity delights in the "good old times" of the past, she lived too interestedly in present and passing events to retain a vivid memory of scenes obscured by the dust of decades. There were, however, a few impressions ineffaceable, among these was her first school experience. The teacher was a phlegmatic person of Dutch lineage, from whom in a few months she learned to "read, write and cipher," a creditable record for a pupil whose instructor was so inefficient as often to sleep in the midst of a recitation, an example which she would humorously say "she had never imitated."

Whilst still young, her parents removed to a section of Abbeville County called "Hard Labor." It would be interesting to know whether this unpromising name originated from a local cause or was bestowed by some discouraged first settler.

Having tasted the fruit of knowledge she was eager "for more," but the elder children had the precedence in such education as their circumstances and the period afforded, on the same principle that the well-preserved garment descended the "stair steps," and the youngest child rarely owned a "brand-new suit" until too large to wear "made over" clothes. These years must have included the time when she "studied with an open book at her side, whilst carding rolls for the spinning wheel," or "parsed a sentence in grammar whilst walking back and forth twisting the thread," an experience referred to when urging her pupils to profit by their exceptional advantage in this regard.

She must have been eighteen years old when both parents in a few weeks of each other died with a malignant fever, for it was previous to their death that her life's romance occurred. Her affection had been won and troth plighted to a young physician practicing in the settlement. Whether his character was objectionable or some other ground of dislike, so it was, that her father strenuously opposed their marriage, and on his death-bed won from her a promise to annul their engagement. Her filial obedience was thus subjected to a severe test and "found *not* wanting." It must, however, have been a trial to her, as their mutual affection was strong. He, too, was both intelligent and cultivated, probably above the average. This is presumed from letters and original poetry which, with the desire for sympathy so natural, she allowed a confidential friend, long after his early death, to read, and which were not inferior, perhaps, to the like effusions of the present cultured age. These, with many precious mementoes of her girlhood, were burned in the hotel at Due West, in 1865.

Her parents after their removal connected themselves with the Associate Reformed Church at Cedar Springs, and though several miles distant the family regularly attended its services. Riding on horseback behind an elder sister or in "the gig" with her mother, the early Sabbath hours found them churchward, and in deprecating the frequent criticism of the present-day-long sermon, she said there might have been, but she did not recollect, complaint or weariness of these Sabbath exercises, although the rays of the setting sun ofttimes mingled with the benediction. The good mother, as was customary excepting on the rigidly observed fast days, always provided lunch. This in summer was discussed with the sermon, both no doubt heartily, in the shade of an adjacent grove ; in winter by fires kindled for comfort and to make coffee for the aged. "Presbyterian bread," from flour or corn meal, was a regular institution, and fried in egg-batter made capital sandwiches. No other "dainty dish" was ever sweeter than these simple lunches, eaten in the intervals of sermons which, without fear or favor, discussed decrees and propounded the strong doctrines of the covenanting faith, all untroubled by the miserable phantasies of "science so called." Stoves were a luxury as yet unconceived. The infirm and invalids sometimes indulged in a hot brick, and but one person, probably the aristocrat, had a perforated tin box in which could be set a cup full of coals.

An incident of these years she sorrowfully recalled. Under her mother's care was an orphan sister, a bright girl much beloved by the family. With youth and health, joyous and bouyant, she on a wintry day engaged in a snow-ball frolic. To escape the pelting of her companions she ran hastily into an out house, slipped and accidentally fell across the "beam" of a loom. A servant who was weaving ran to her aid, found that she had fainted, and called for assistance ; but the efforts of friends and physicians were unavailing, even to restore consciousness, and in a brief period she died. This terrible shock was a life remembrance.

The death of her parents and marriage of her elder brother and sisters left herself and younger brother alone in the old homestead. The interval in which they thus lived, she recalled with pleasure, and we may presume that with characteristic fidelity she "kept house." Whether she was as yet a communicant, or when and under whose ministry she united with the church, we do not and can not now know ; but probably not, as she was fond of the social dance and other worldly amusements, though disliking and rarely participating in the somewhat rude "plays" then "the fashion."

The marriage of this brother released her from this duty, and with the thirst for knowledge unquenched she decided to utilize her small inherited property in securing such education as would enable her to become self-supporting as a teacher. A portion of this had been unfortunately lost, nor was this her only similar experience. She lived to see the earnings of her life, of which not a penny was stained by the "rust which corrupts," all swept away through misplaced trust, and, thus impoverished, her latter end pecuniarily was smaller than its beginning.

She had relatives and friends at Newberry C. H., and thither she went, resolved to "make the most" of such opportunity for culture as could there be obtained. In the school and family of Dr. Samuel Pressly, a distinguished educator, who afterwards occupied the President's chair in the University of Georgia, she was received as pupil and boarder. Here she found congenial friends, and in Dr. Pressly a mentor, for whom she ever retained a grateful regard. How few are thus favored—to hold a warm place in the heart of a pupil for more than sixty years!

In a class of boys who were being prepared for College, and of other girls, she studied Latin, mathematics, &c., and with pardonable vanity, inasmuch as it demonstrated what was then scarcely within the pale of argument, she recalled the class-marks, most creditable to her sex, therefore a reliable proof that, *mentally, they* were not so very inferior.

An incident grim and tragic, but illustrative of "the way they did things in those days," she sometimes described in an impressive manner, and with something of the "bated breath" with which, under favorable surroundings, a shadowed room, an eerie wind, and appreciative listeners, a wierd ghost-tale should be related. It seems that a man of good family and some wealth had committed an atrocious murder. He was found guilty and condemned. Dr. Pressly was appointed by the authorities, or selected by himself, as his spiritual guide and comforter, in this dreadful strait. On the day of his execution, a bleak, inclement day, Dr. Pressly preached his funeral in the village court house, to an immense throng, the Doctor's own family and pupils, as also the friends of the doomed man being present. Draped in his shroud, and shivering with mortal terror, the victim listened attentively to his own funeral discourse, knowing that each word as it fell, represented a moment of the few remaining to him, ere launched into the awful realities of eternity. Although sick with the horror of the scene, it had a fearful fascination, and albeit unwillingly, she took in every detail. Her last glimpse of the criminal, as with Dr. Pressly, and seated on his own coffin, he was driven through the surging crowd, was ineffaceable. Many women, as well as a multitude of men, flocked to the place of execution, and she "was glad that their own party were surfeited with the ghastly tragedy, and decided to return to their home."

This was but an episode in the otherwise *happy* period of her "school days," as hundreds who have passed from her tuition have heard, and themselves experienced, when their own class books were closed, to be replaced by those in which are engraved life's sterner lessons.

When her purse was nearly depleted, Miss McQuerns, through her friend, James Fair, Esq., secured a school near his home at "Fair's Bridge," in Abbeville County. This was probably in 1829. So efficient was she in this first attempt, as to leave an abiding impress upon persons yet living, who here enjoyed the benefit of her "prentice" teaching.

In 1832 her life-long friend and relative, Capt. Wm. T. Drennan, secured for her a promising field at Mt. Carmel, a small village but a short distance from the then celebrated Willington school. Her first year here was in an "old field school house," excepting that it was embowered in a grove of hickory and chestnut trees, with a luxuriant undergrowth of the huckleberry, all of which were a "joy" to the scholars, only from the advantage which the sprouts afforded her in the application of that instrument, so earnestly recommended by "the wisest man," the which she literally interpreted and conscientiously applied. Her first examination here was held in Zoar Methodist church. Around the box-pulpit was erected a platform, on which were seated distinguished persons, amongst whom was Dr. Moses Waddel, the veteran teacher, and his sons, with others, whose fame has and will survive when their mortal remains shall have dissolved into their native element. This occasion, although not so *recherche*, was no doubt as enjoyable, and afforded her as much solid satisfaction as the Commencements of her latter years. Dr. Waddell opened the exercises with prayer, and closed them with a congratulatory address, in which he said : "I have attended many examinations, but have never seen such progress in so short a time." From the feeble lips of a friend whose age approximates her own, these facts are obtained. She had found her vocation and was thenceforth wedded to it.

So encouraged were the trustees of this school with its prospects and condition, that they purchased a large and more comfortable building, with a hall, piazza, and several rooms. In the meantime, her weeks of vacation were spent in the city of Augusta, Ga., and there utilized in the improvement of her knowledge of music and drawing.

Under the present flattering prospect, she allowed herself the joy of one of her life's benefactions. An orphan neice, Miss Sarah Ann McQuerns, was sent for, whose expense of boarding, education, &c., she thenceforth assumed, until her marriage with Rev. Mr. Millen, in 1841, released her from this responsibility. This neice was a pious and lovely girl. Their mutual attachment was strong, and the death of Mrs. Millen a few months after marriage was a sorrow. After more than forty years, have they not met and recalled the affectionate association of this period?

The next session of her school brought such an influx of pupils that she found it necessary to employ an assistant, Rev. Isaac Waddell, then pastor of Willington church, and with increasing reputation and influence, scattering with lavish hand the seeds of immortelles both in Carolina and Georgia, she abided under this "vine" of her own culture for the succeeding seven years.

But the responsibility of so large a school and the overwork consequent injured her health, and at the expiration of this period her resignation was reluctantly accepted, and she returned to Fair's Bridge, where in the family of Esq. Fair she resided for a year as guest and governess.

Then she came to Due West, which place from thenceforth was a sort of Mecca to her, or an "ark" to which from her absences she returned "as a dove to its window." Here she remained for an interval, teaching in an academy adjoining the church lot. Probably, too, it was about this time that she seized the opportunity of a Synodical meeting in Tennessee to accompany some friends who were delegates, on a visit to her sisters, there resident, and spent a year with them. Both of these sisters were in such circumstances as to have made her very comfortable in their homes, and they insisted upon her remaining with them. But she preferred "to eat the bread of her own earning," and gratefully but firmly declined. They then offered to secure for her a school very near to them; but "the climate was too bleak," and she longed for the sunny warmth of her native State. Her's was the experience of so many Carolinians who, in the language of that eloquent minister, Dr. Palmer, "In all their wanderings breathe no more fervent prayer than in death to sleep upon her faithful bosom until the awful day." Thenceforth, whatsoever was Carolina's destiny, whether overwhelmed by the dire calamities of war or springing Phœnix like from the ashes of its dead hopes, it was for her a "good enough home, in which to live, to die, and be buried."

On her return she accepted a school on Hard Labor, principally induced thereto by the opportunity of educating the children of a neice. In 1847 she again returned to Mt. Carmel, where she remained three years; thence to Due West, where she taught a full school until 1853. In the meantime the Presbyterian Female College at Anderson C. H., under the care of Rev. Ebenezer Pressly, formerly President of Erskine College, was acquiring repute, and she accepted his invitation to become assistant teacher therein. In this pleasant village she formed, as elsewhere, warm and abiding friendships, and established in her vocation that "good name" which is "better than precious ointment." After Dr. Pressly's resignation, she remained in this college some years, in connection with Rev. A. A. Morse, Rev. J. O. Lindsay, and probably Rev. Samuel Jones of the Methodist Church, winning the esteem of her associate teachers and the affection of her pupils, one of whom recently remarked, "No one but my mother ever had so much to do in moulding my character as my beloved friend and teacher, Miss McQuerns."

From Anderson our friend returned to Due West. The school here was assuming a larger area of usefulness, and in 1859 a meeting of the citizens was held, in which it was determined to give it a more permanent organization. Liberal subscriptions were received, the erection of a suitable building begun, a competent faculty elected, Miss McQuerns among the number, and a charter secured for the Due West Female College.

Classes were organized in the Fall of this year, and from that auspicious day until her death she was an honored, though latter-ly, from her age and infirmities, rather an honorary, member of the Faculty. Until 1866 she was Principal of the Primary Department; afterwards teacher of Astronomy, Botany, and the ornamental branches. How many will recall the pleasant hours of some cloudless night, when surrounded by her class—a galaxy of more intrinsic worth, because of its immortal capacities, than Orion or Pleiades—she would trace the constellations and "call them by their names." Or, on some bright spring day, accompany the Botany class in a search for wild flowers, and with unwearied patience analyze and explain, though their youthful exuberance doubtless found more pleasure in the fresh air and glowing exercise than in the drier fields of Botanical research. "A thing of beauty" was a "joy" to her, whether in the "heavens above or the earth beneath," whether artistic or the more humble creation of unskilled hands. And as she grew aged and deaf, and her inability for active service increased, she found in "fancy work" a congenial employment. Mementoes of her taste and the skill of her trembling, wrinkled fingers, are found in scores of homes.

In the family of James Lindsay, Esq., who was a devoted friend and benefactor of Erskine (male) College, she boarded, with the exception of a few months, during all of her residence in Due West, and their mutual esteem was strong. But, one by one, she saw them pass away; the parents and six children, leaving to perpetuate his honored name, only the elder and youngest brothers of all this household, whom she found so happy and promising. With the widowed mother she mourned when her brave boys were brought from the battle-fields of Virginia. By the side of husband and children she saw this bereaved mother laid, and Mrs. Dr. Bonner, the only daughter, and her beloved pupil and friend, after a space, went to join the family circle. Her brothers and sisters, her dear relative Capt. Drennan, and, with few exceptions, all the friends of her youth, had now gone "beyond the river." Ah, how desolate is the feeling, that in all the world there's not ONE left to call the familiar given name.

Other troubles, too, beset her. Whilst sojourning for a few months at the hotel, during the dark days which followed the war, it was burned by an incendiary, and she, with others, were only saved by leaping from an upper balcony, upon mattresses held to receive them. Clothing, books and valuables were all consumed, and to add to her discomfort she was notified of the loss elsewhere of some thousands of dollars, on which she depended to tide her comfortably, and independently, through the extreme age on which she was entering. Yet, in all this she "sinned not." "I have been young, and now am old, yet have I not seen the righteous forsaken, nor his seed begging bread." This was her assured hope, nor was it misplaced. "The barrel of meal" did not "waste" nor the "cruse of oil fail" until the day on which she entered into an heavenly inheritance.

Her seventy-fifth year was celebrated by what thereafter constituted an annual holiday and season of social pleasure in the College, viz., a birth-day dinner, accompanied by the presentation of "gifts" from friends, in and out of the College, particularly the associate teachers and the senior class of young ladies. Although deeply grateful for these exhibitions of esteem, yet with a characteristic independence which shrank from obligation, and a humility, the last to recognize her own worth, it was almost, if not quite, with a feeling of self-denial that she suffered herself to become the honored guest of these festivals, the last of which, with more than usual pleasure, occurred on March 8, 1886.

The death of Dr. Bonner, President of the College, was a sorrowful event to her, as well as to the Institution. We are tempted here to pay a just tribute to this eminent man, whose loss, to church and school, to society and home, is so deeply felt and sincerely lamented, but forbear. Under his wise and nurturing government, assisted by an excellent corps of teachers, the College doors had been opened, wide and invitingly, to throngs of intelligent school-girls, and with assured reputation it had become a power for good. She had here retained her position, whilst teachers and pupils, year by year, had come and gone, some to their life-work, some to the grave. And when this her unwavering friend was "touched by the finger of God and died," she "mourned." Tears from the dim eyes of age, and smiles from its pallid, trembling lips, are alike scant and pitiful ; but hers was that perennial heart which can "rejoice with them that do rejoice, and weep with them that weep."

In this trouble, as personally affected, she patiently bided, calling to remembrance her life-long "songs in the night." Though "lover and friend hast thou put far from me and mine acquaintance into darkness," yet "in the Lord do I put my trust." He is my God, my "times are in his hand." So from this strait she was again removed into a "large place," and the path for her tottering feet was smoothed.

The death of Dr. Bonner necessitated a re-organization of the Faculty, in which Prof. J. P. Kennedy was elected President, and Mrs. Kate P. Kennedy and Mrs. Lila M. Bonner, vice-Principals. These all, were devoted friends of Miss McQuerns. Mrs. Kennedy had been her pupil, and revered her as a mother. Her resignation which, recognizing her failing capacities, she then, and repeatedly thereafter tendered, was not accepted; Mr. Kennedy assuring her, with other cheering words, that he considered her example and prayers in behalf of the College, of more benefit than the service of its most efficient teacher. And was he mistaken? The influence of such a person, who can estimate? It leaves ineffaceable traces on the shores of time, but its real fruitage is stored in the garners of eternity. To these friends, and others of the Faculty, for all their unwearied kindness, which undoubtedly prolonged her life, in behalf of the thousands in whose homes her name is a "household word," and for myself, to whom was granted the precious privilege of ministering to her, as, day by day, she drew nearer the foot of the hill, I would here express sincere gratitude.

I have spoken elsewhere of her piety. In this regard she was a "living epistle." Devotedly attached to the Associate Reformed Presbyterian Church, of which she was a member, yet her catholic spirit included in its love all who "name the name of Jesus." In every "good word and work" she was interested. Through her efforts the Ladies Benevolent Society of this place originated, and at her instigation letters were written throughout the church urging such organizations. Their successful operation is a congratulation to all who are interested in the philanthropy of the period, whether in home or foreign fields. In the establishment of a W. C. T. U. at this place she exerted herself, even in her great weakness, and rejoiced in the reports of the influence for good that woman is exerting in this great question. Foreign missions claimed its place in her heart. The first missionary sent forth by her church, Mrs. Giffen, nee Miss Mary Galloway, was her pupil and loving friend, with whom she corresponded, and for whom she prayed until the death of Mrs. Giffen, in Egypt, blighted her bright promise of usefulness in that benighted land.

In her benefactions Miss McQuerns was phenomenally generous. "Give to him that asketh of thee, and from him that would borrow of thee turn not thou away," was a rule, the literal observance of which in her last decade, and with her weakened judgment, became so impoverishing that her friends, as far as was just and right, exerted themselves to shield her from the importunities of the impecunious. Unworthily as was her beneficence sometimes bestowed, yet acting from such a principle, the "bread upon the waters" was returned her "many fold."

From all this we may gather these traits of her spiritual character—that its distinctive features were, unswerving trust in God, a supreme loyalty to the Word of God, constancy and fidelity in the public and private worship of God, and a desire amounting to zeal to co-operate in all schemes for the promotion of the wellbeing of humanity. "To do good and to communicate" was her great delight. Her motto, "Trust in the Lord and do good," and its promise she literally experienced, "So shalt thou dwell in the land and verily thou shalt be fed." The "straight path" was to her the plainest, and it was a wonder and an impatience that the "by-ways" were so thronged.

But the shadows increased, "her strength became weariness," and "the grasshopper a burden." "Tired, so tired," was often the pathetic plaint which mingled with this thank-acknowledgment so familiar to her lips, "Goodness and mercy have followed me all the days of my life." In the bloom of her youth she had become, in its Christlike significance, a "little child." With the approach of age she recognized its inevitable tendency, struggled for a time against it, and then patiently submitted to the weakness of the "second childhood." In this sorrowful stage of life the guilelessness of infancy was so manifest, as to win admiration, even amid the pathetic notes of the loosening "silver chords."

Her attacks of debility now became frequent, and without disease, or pain, the fountain of life ran low. But the watchful care of friends was blessed in a repeated reaction, and with returning strength came assiduous application to her employments, these principally consisting in making of various mementoes for friends, the completion of which she felt would be the last she could undertake.

On Monday, May 11, 1886, whilst moulding wax to finish up some sprigs of flowers for the teachers and senior class, as a slight return for their kindness on her preceding birth-day, she contracted a cold. Tuesday she remained in her room, but was so much recovered on Wednesday as to insist on going to College that she might meet this class, and herself present to them these tokens of her handiwork. Their absence from College, in the composition of Commencement essays, was a disappointment, and she returned home prostrated and very indisposed. During the night asthma developed. It was not a severe attack, there was no acute pain, only the distress of short breathing; yet "so slight was her experience of aches and pains" that she felt that this was beyond her strength of endurance. This distress continued in a greater or less degree through her illness, and th unremitting attention of friends, and the skill of physicians could scarcely alleviate it. With no acute pain, and no fever, or abnormal pulse, or threatening symptom, the "wheel" at the "cistern" was surely shattering, and we felt that prayer and effort would alike unavail to retain her from the "long home." Her distress through all her illness was permeated with the submissiveness of the christian. "Though He slay me, yet will I trust in Him." "It is the Lord, let Him do what seemeth Him good." "I know that my Redeemer liveth." And with many other beautiful promises and portions did she comfort herself. Scripture reading and prayer were a delight, and her own petitions almost unceasing. For hours would she pray, striving to recollect every person and object, recalling again and again some beloved one, and pleading in their behalf. Psalms and hymns . were often too repeated. The twenty-third Psalm and the hymn, "How firm a foundation, ye saints of the Lord," she for many years was in the habit of repeating just before sleeping. I should have mentioned elsewhere that her regular order of Scripture reading was, ten chapters each in the Old and New Testaments every Sabbath, and a portion every morning of the week.

On the evening of May the 26th she was more comfortable, and with the desire to console one whose sorrowful countenance she noticed, she smiled and said, "Don't grieve, I will stay with you until to-morrow evening." And knowing our anxiety to stimulate her lost appetite she asked for coffee. Afterwards took both tonic and stimulant, and then with a sigh as of relief said, "Now let me sleep," and in a few moments was slumbering as sweetly and calmly as an infant. This was unbroken until midnight, the hour for her medicine, and as her pulse continued good we hoped it would prove beneficial. But the attempt to arouse her was vain, and in a short time she, who had "all her life been subject to bondage through fear of death," unconsciously passed the dark valley and entered upon her reward, May 27, 1886.

It was past the middle watches and she slept,
    Was it a dream?
That she stood upon the shelving brink
    Of Jordan's fearful stream?
Trembling stood, until the angel Azrael spake
    These words of cheer :
Child of God ! I'll bear thee safely through the waters !
    Do not fear !

On the other side One met her, lovingly.
    Is it a dream?
And He pointed to the soul-home,
    Blazing in its glory gleam.
Led her up a starry pathway
    Till the jeweled gates were passed.
Dreaming ! Joy, oh, joy ineffable.
    Awake, in heaven at last !

"And, lo ! as she entered she was transfigured, and she had raiment put on her that shone like gold. There were also that met, with harp and crown, and gave them to her—the harp to praise withal, and the crown in token of honor ; and all the bells in the city rang again for joy, as it was said unto her, 'Enter into the joy of your Lord.' "

Very tender was the chill hand which smoothed from her care-worn face its many furrows and left a halo of peace upon her aged brow.

Covered with floral tributes, after an appropriate funeral service, her remains were deposited in the cemetery of the Associate Reformed Presbyterian church at Due West, where the sound of both church and college bells will often reverberate, but never again recall her to the worship of the one, or the service of the other.

"I hope I may die in warm weather, and not in the bleak, inclement winter." This was often, latterly, an expressed desire. She so loved sunshine and brightness, and probably deprecated for others the discomfort of the season in the necessary watching and attention of illness, death and burial. But her "time" was in an indulgent Father's hand, and He made it subservient to her wish. On a balmy May night, a very gem in its cloudless beauty, she left us, and went to be for ever with the Lord.

"That where I am there ye
May also come to me."
Not as a mournful dole,
Accepted doubtingly,
But gladly she received
This message of His word,
In all its glorious heights and depths,
"Forever with the Lord."

Beyond, it may be far
Yon constellated dome,
Or very near to earth
The portals of this home ;
Yet there's a place "prepared,"
Such is his blessed word,
Where will be garnered all His own,
"Forever with the Lord."

Saints of all ages there,
A great unnumber'd throng ;
What will it be to hear
And join their glad "new song"?
The matchless song of grace,
To tell its numbers o'er,
And 'neath the radiance of His face
Abide forevermore.

Kindred and precious friends
Are with that ransomed host,
Those that with us she mourned,
The loved and early lost ;
Lost ! It is only ours,
That sorrow-laden word.
Ye're safe, beloved ; O, happy lot,
"Forever with the Lord."

Faithful and true in life,
Faithful unto the end ;
O, that, like one of old,
Her mantle might desend.
Full-sheaved, at eventide,
She went to her reward,
A spotless robe, a jewelled crown,
"Forever with the Lord."

Gates of pure pearl and gold,
  Bright mansions of the blest,
Somewhere within your fold
  She's found her longed-for rest ;
Close to the great white throne,
  Near by the crystal sea,
Friend of my life, thou'rt "with the Lord,"
  Through all eternity !

This simple chronicle, friends, is now before you. It has been written as tenderly and ingenuously as if "face to face" in her own little room, so hallowed by prayer and praise, a very Penial indeed, we had met together and talked of "these things." And have I in aught exaggerated or even told the half?

May we learn as she did the christian's secret of a happy life, that life which is "hid with Christ in God," so that "when Christ who is our life shall appear then shall we also appear with him in glory."

⊹ TRIBUTES OF RESPECT ⊹

———o———

FACULTY OF DUE WEST FEMALE COLLEGE.

Resolutions in reference to the death of Miss ELIZABETH McQUERNS adopted by the Faculty of the Due West Female College :

WHEREAS, It has pleased our heavenly Father to remove from our midst Miss ELIZABETH McQUERNS ; and, whereas, we know He doeth what He may with his own, and whatsoever he doeth is right ; therefore resolved,

1. That we bow in humble submission to that dispensation of Providence that removes from our sight our venerable and beloved friend.

2. That the College with which she has been identified during its whole history, has lost a faithful and conscientious teacher ; our community the living examplification of the beauty and power of a holy life ; the poor and distressed a sympathizing and unfailing friend ; the church and all its enterprises an earnest and generous supporter.

3. And while we must mourn our irreparable loss, we feel grateful for the pleasing assurance we are permitted to cherish, that for her to depart was far better, and that she has gone to "the mountain of myrrh, and to the hill of frankincense, till the day break and the shadows flee away."

4. That we mingle our tears with those friends, scattered all over this Southern land, to whom the name of Miss McQUERNS is as ointment poured forth, and who mourn, most of all, because they shall see her face no more.

5. That we cherish her memory as a priceless heritage, and that we imitate the noble example she has set before us, inasmuch as throughout her whole life she has quietly and consistently followed the footsteps of her Divine Master, that she has gone about doing good, and has lived, not for herself alone, but for all those whom God has made her neighbors.

6. That the *Associate Reformed Presbyterian* be requested to publish these resolutions, and the Abbeville papers to copy them.

AMELIAN LITERARY SOCIETY OF DUE WEST FEMALE COLLEGE.

Resolutions adopted by the Amelian Literary Society of the Due West Female College :

WHEREAS, It has pleased God in his providence to remove from our midst our faithful and venerable teacher, Miss ELIZABETH McQUERNS, who has for so many years been the stay of our Institution ; resolved,

1. That we have sustained an irreparable loss in the death of this beloved friend.

2. That we recognize the merciful hand of Providence in this our great bereavement, and bow in humble submission to His divine will.

3. That we will endeavor to heed his noble counsels, imitate her true womanly character, and keep fresh the memory of this consistent Christian.

4. That we will wear, until the expiration of the session, the usual badge of mourning, as a feeble indication of our inexpressible reverence for our departed friend.

5. That we will devote a page to her memory in the records of our Society.

6. That we respectfully request the publication of these resolutions in the *Associate Reformed Presbyterian* and the County papers.

FACULTY OF ERSKINE COLLEGE.

WHEREAS, It has pleased the sovereign Disposer of all things to remove from us by death that illustrious teacher and eminent Christian, Miss ELIZABETH McQUERNS ; therefore resolved,

1. That we humbly submit to the will of Him who doeth well—the Lord gave and the Lord hath taken away ; blessed be the name of the Lord.

2. That in her death the cause of education has lost one of its ablest and mots zealous friends, and the youth of both sexes their safest counselor, and the brightest example of a sanctified, educated life.

3. That as an expression of our respect for her memory, we adjourn the College for the remainder of the day after the exercises of this morning.

4. That a copy of these resolutions be published in the *Associate Reformed Presbyterian.*

LADIES' MISSIONARY SOCIETY.

At a meeting of the Ladies Missionary Society of Due West the following preamble and resolutions were adopted :

WHEREAS, God in his providence has been pleased to remove from a sphere of usefulness and honor in our midst our much esteemed and beloved colaborer, Miss ELIZABETH McQUERNS, a most active and influential member of our Society (the originator of it, and in that way the originator of other Societies throughout Synod), who, we all have every reason to believe, was ready and patiently waiting for the summons of her divine Master, and that she is now enjoying the fullness of the presence of Him she so delighted to serve Him here below ; therefore be it resolved,

1. That we regard this as a sad deprivation and an afflictive loss to us as a Society and as christian friends.

2. That we will best manifest respect to the memory of her whose loss we deplore by endeavoring to imitate her example and by cultivating those lovely qualities which rendered her so dear to us, and which was so greatly esteemed by all who knew her.

3. That we will cherish her memory for her almsdeeds, her benevolence, her sympathy with the poor and afflicted, her prayers, her deep solicitude for the welfare of those who were afar off as well as for those near her.

4. That we express our thanks to Almighty God for raising up and continuing among us so long one who seemed to fill the picture of a "handmaid of the Lord."

5. That we bow with humble submission to that mysterious Providence which doeth all things for the good of his own people.

6. That a page in our Minute book be inscribed to her memory.

7. That a copy of these resolutions be published in the *Associate Reformed Presbyterian.*

www.ingramcontent.com/pod-product-compliance
Lightning Source LLC
Chambersburg PA
CBHW020707260626
47157CB00008B/3181